Jordan's Football

Story by Jenny Giles   Illustrations by Al Fiorentino

Jordan's dad said,
"I'm going for a run
around the park.
Then I will come back
and play football with you."

Jordan kicked the ball to Kris.

Kris kicked it back,

and it went over

by some trees.

Jordan ran to get it.

But a big boy got the ball first.

"This is a good football,"

he said to his friends.

"Let's go and play with it."

"That is **my** football!" said Jordan.

"You can't take it away!"

The boy laughed.

"Who is going to stop us?" he said.

"My dad will stop you," said Jordan.

"He is here in the park."

The boy laughed.

"No, he is not!" he said.

"You can't trick us!"

Kris looked around
for Jordan's dad.
He saw some men
running into the park.

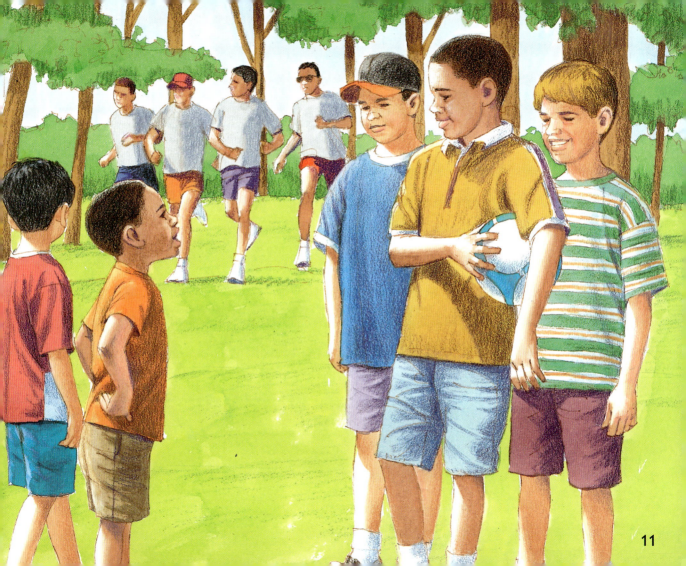

Kris said to Jordan,

"**Look!**

Here come your dad's friends!"

The boy laughed again.

"Don't play tricks on us," he said.

"You can't have your football back."

13

Then one of the men called out, "Hello, Jordan! Is your dad here?"

"Yes!" shouted Jordan.
"He is running around the park."

The big boy put the ball down and ran off with his friends.

15

"You got your football back!" said Kris.

"And I was not playing a trick at all," laughed Jordan.